The Real Book of
FIRST STORIES

Illustrated by June Goldsborough

ISBN   0-528-82190-3
ISBN   0-528-82191-1 (lib. bdg.)
Copyright © 1973 by Rand McNally & Company
All rights reserved
Library of Congress Catalog Card Number: 73-7200
Printed in the United States of America
by Rand McNally & Company
First printing, 1973
Second printing, 1976

Ⓐ RAND McNALLY & COMPANY
Chicago   New York   San Francisco

WHICH STORY?

"A story," says your small listener, bringing THE REAL BOOK OF FIRST STORIES to you. "Read a story."

And you, the reader, with this new book—or with a child who is not yet accustomed to being read to—wonder which story. Which to hold attention? Which to, in some way, entertain or enrich this small person? Which to, perhaps, identify an experience or an emotion, or to lead to some new understanding? In general, two simple guidelines can be followed.

Read to the child as soon as he shows interest, even though "reading" may mean no more than looking at the pictures together. This is a vital first step to a later interest in books of all kinds.

At first, suit the length of the story to the age of the listener. Choose a very short story or poem for the younger child and a longer one with more plot, greater suspense, for the older child. The youngest child will probably respond best to just those stories indicated as appropriate for his age level. The older child, however, can be expected to like not only those stories indicated for his age group but to like stories keyed to the interests of much younger children as well. The stories in this book are, then, rated upwards from the youngest levels.

●For the youngest children (some 2-year-olds, the 3's and 4's): *Look at Me, Mamma; Zoo Riders; Hello, Sun; When I Am a Bear; Erik and Red and the Store;* and *Molli and Mrs. Neighbor.*

■For the middle group (the 4- and 5-year-olds): Those stories in the preceding group as well as *Little Red Riding Hood; The Three Bears; The Three Little Pigs; The Little Red Hen; The Girl Who Wanted To Be a Little Red Hen;* and *I Went to the Zoo in the Rain.*

▲For the oldest group (some 5-year-olds, the 6's and 7's): Stories in the preceding two groups and *Just Old Enough; The 621 Friends of Aaron Zee; Henry and Mr. Bear;* and *Romper, Tromper, Stomper, and Boo.*

As the child becomes acquainted with the stories herein, you'll find guidelines quite unnecessary, for he'll happily and satisfactorily choose stories that are right for his age and stage of development.

Now, take your cue from your listener: Enjoy a story!

CONTENTS

● For the Youngest Group (some 2's, the 3's and 4's).

▪ For the Middle Group (the 4's and 5's).
Children in this age group will also enjoy stories for younger children.

▲ For the Oldest Group (some 5's, the 6's and 7's).
Children in this age group will also enjoy stories listed in the two preceding groups.

Look at Me, Mamma!

by GEDA BRADLEY MATHEWS

When a little beetle digs a hole in the ground, he says,
   "Look at me, Mamma!" And she does.

When a little roly-poly bug somersaults around, he says,
   "Look at me, Mamma!" And she does.

When a little grasshopper jumps over a twig,
When a little ant picks up something big,
When a little ladybug swings on a sprout,
When a little spider learns to help out, they say,
   "Look at me, Mamma!" And their mammas do.

Yes, and when a little water bug ducks his whole face,
   he says, "Look at me, Mamma!" And she does.

When a little cricket makes music everyplace (wonderful
rackety music), he says, "Look at me, Mamma!" And she does.

And when you

Dig a hole in the ground and turn somersaults all around—
when you jump over a twig and pick up something big—when you
learn to swing and to help out and to duck your face (your whole
face)—and when you make wonderful rackety music everyplace,
do you say, "Look at me, Mamma!" And does she?

Does she give you a hug? And do you glow all over like
a lightning bug?

9

Molli and Mrs. Neighbor

A Toddler's Tale by BETTY KENT

Molli is a little girl with red hair and freckles.

She lives with her Mamma and Daddy and her doll Judy in a red-brick house on a hill.

Next door is another red-brick house. Once upon a time, nobody lived there.

Nobody for Molli and Judy to play with.

One day Molli and Judy watched a moving van bring furniture to the house next door.

Molli saw a pretty lady go to the front door.

"That's our new neighbor," Mamma said.

"Let's go see Mrs. Neighbor," Molli said.

After the moving van left, Molli, Mamma, and Judy took a plate of cookies to Mrs. Neighbor.

"Where's *your* little girl?" Molli asked Mrs. Neighbor.

"I don't have a little girl," Mrs. Neighbor said. "Would you like to be my little girl, too?"

"I like you," Molli said. She and Judy sat on Mrs. Neighbor's lap.

After a while, Molli, Mamma, and Judy went home so Mrs. Neighbor could put her things away.

The next morning Molli saw Mrs. Neighbor in a little red car.

The little red car zoomed down the driveway.

After a while, the little red car zoomed back up the driveway.

Molli and Judy went out to play after lunch.

Along the side of Mrs. Neighbor's house were some pretty flowers.

Molli pulled up a red one to give to Mrs. Neighbor.

"Oh, dear," said Mrs. Neighbor when Molli gave her the red flower. "That's the petunia I just planted. Let's put it back. It'll grow and have more flowers."

"More flowers," said Molli.

Mrs. Neighbor dug a hole with a spade from the garage. She held the plant in the hole.

"Will you put the dirt around it?" she asked Molli.

Molli patted the dirt around the petunia.

"Would you like a flower garden of your very own?" asked Mrs. Neighbor.

"A flower garden just for Molli and Judy," said Molli.

Molli's Mamma let Molli and Judy go with Mrs. Neighbor to the Flower Market.

Molli picked out pansies for her garden.

When Daddy came home, he spaded a place in the yard for the pansies.

Mamma held the flowers while Molli put the dirt around them.

Now Molli had a flower garden like Mrs. Neighbor's. It was fun being Mrs. Neighbor's little girl, too.

The Three Little Pigs

as told by HELEN KRONBERG OLSON

Once upon a time, an old mother pig and her three little pigs lived together in a very small house.

One day the first little pig thought it was time he went out into the world.

"You may go," said Mother Pig. "But be sure and build a strong house so that the wolf cannot get in."

"I will," said the little pig. Then off he went down the road.

He walked uphill and downhill until he came to a man with a load of straw.

"Would you like to buy some straw?" asked the man.

"Yes," said the little pig. "It would be easy to build a house of straw."

So he bought the straw and built a house with it.

After a while the wolf came along. He walked right up to the house of straw and knocked on the door.

The little pig went to the window and looked out. There stood the wolf!

"Little pig, little pig, let me come in," said the wolf.

"No, by the hair of my chinny-chin-chin. You are the wolf, and you can't come in," said the little pig.

"Then I'll huff and I'll puff, and I'll blow your house in," said the wolf.

But the little pig would not open the door.

So the wolf huffed and he puffed, and he blew the house in.

Then he grabbed the little pig and took him home with him. "When you are fattened up," said the wolf, "you will make a good Sunday dinner."

Now the second little pig went out into the world.

He walked uphill and downhill until he came to a man with a load of sticks.

"Would you like to buy some sticks?" asked the man.

"Yes," said the little pig. "It would be quite easy to build a house of sticks."

So he bought the sticks and built a house with them.

After a while the wolf came along. He walked right up to the house of sticks and knocked on the door.

The little pig went to the window and looked out. There stood the wolf!

"Little pig, little pig, let me come in," said the wolf.

"No, by the hair of my chinny-chin-chin. You are the wolf, and you can't come in," said the little pig.

"Then I'll huff and I'll puff, and I'll blow your house in," said the wolf.

But the little pig would not open the door.

So the wolf huffed and he puffed, and he blew the house in.

Then he grabbed the little pig and took him home with him. "When you are fattened up," said the wolf, "you will make a good Sunday dinner."

Now the third little pig went out into the world.

He walked uphill and downhill until he came to a man with a load of bricks.

"Would you like to buy some bricks?" asked the man.

"Yes," said the little pig. "It won't be easy to build a house of bricks, but it will be a strong house."

So he bought the bricks and built a house with them.

After a while the wolf came along. He walked right up to the house of bricks and knocked on the door.

The little pig went to the window and looked out. There stood the wolf!

"Little pig, little pig, let me come in," said the wolf.

"No, by the hair of my chinny-chin-chin. You are the wolf, and you can't come in," said the little pig.

"Then I'll huff and I'll puff, and I'll blow your house in," said the wolf.

But the little pig would not open the door.

So the wolf huffed and he puffed, and he puffed and he huffed, but he could not blow the house in.

Now the wolf thought of a trick to get the little pig out of his house.

"The apples are ripe in the orchard," said the wolf. "I will come for you tomorrow morning and we will get some apples."

"What time will you come?" asked the little pig.

"At six o'clock," said the wolf.

But the little pig went to the orchard at five o'clock. He picked a basket of ripe apples. Then he went home.

At six o'clock the wolf came to the little pig's house.

"Come out, little pig," said the wolf. "And we will go to the orchard."

"Thank you," said the little pig. "But I've already been there."

Now the wolf became very angry. But he had to think of another trick.

"There is a fair in the town," said the wolf. "I will take you there in the morning."

"What time will you come?" asked the little pig.

"At five o'clock," said the wolf.

But the little pig went to the fair at four o'clock.

At the fair he bought a fine churn. "This churn will make good butter," he said. "But now I must hurry home before the wolf comes."

Then off he went.

When he got as far as the top of the hill he looked down. And there, halfway up the hill, was the wolf!

The little pig did not waste any time. He got into the churn. And away he rolled down the hill.

The wolf did not know it was the little pig in the churn. "What terrible beast is this?" he said. And he jumped to one side so that he would not be run over.

The churn stopped at the foot of the hill.

And the little pig got out and ran into his house.

When the wolf saw the little pig he became very, very angry.

He climbed up on the roof of the little pig's house. "I will come down the chimney," said the wolf. "And I will eat you right up."

"Come if you wish," said the little pig. Now, as it happened, the smart little pig had a great big wolf-sized pot of water bubbling over the fire in the fireplace.

The wolf came down the chimney. KERSPLASH! He landed in the hot water.

You may be sure that from then on he did not bother any more little pigs.

The third little pig then went to the wolf's house and let the other two little pigs loose. And the three little pigs lived together happily ever after in the strong brick house the third little pig had built.

Romper, Tromper, Stomper, and Boo

by JUDITH ANDERSON

Once upon a time, not too long ago, in a jungle not too far away, lived four elephants named Romper, Tromper, Stomper, and Boo.

Now, Romper was called Romper because when he would walk through the jungle, he would go ROMP ROMP ROMP ROMP, and all the animals who lived in the jungle would hear him ROMP ROMP ROMPing through the jungle, and they would call to one another, "Here comes Romper." And that's the way Romper got his name.

Tromper was called Tromper because when she would walk through the jungle, she would go TROMP TROMP TROMP TROMP, and the animals who lived in the jungle would hear her TROMP TROMP TROMPing through the jungle, and they would call to one another, "Oh, here comes Tromper." And so Tromper was given the name Tromper.

Stomper was named Stomper because when he would walk through the jungle, he would go STOMP STOMP STOMP STOMP, and the animals in the jungle would hear him STOMP STOMP STOMPing through the jungle, and they would say to one another, "Yes, that's Stomper." So Stomper was given the name Stomper.

But when Boo went walking through the jungle, she didn't make any noise at all, and because she didn't make any noise at all, no one ever heard her coming. In fact, the animals usually didn't know Boo was near until she was right beside them. Then she would say, "Boo," because she didn't want to frighten them, and they would jump and say, "BOO!" So Boo was given the name Boo.

The four elephants were very good friends and would often play together in the jungle. One day, while they were playing hide-and-seek, the monkeys and the parrots came speeding through the treetops, crying, "Oh, *terrible*, terrible, terrible, terrible!"

Romper, Tromper, Stomper, and Boo stopped their game and asked what was so very terrible.

"It's men! Strange men! In our jungle!" cried and twittered and screamed the monkeys and parrots. "And they are building traps! Elephant traps!"

"Elephant traps! In our jungle?" said Romper. "This calls for a conference." And the four elephants gathered together for the conference (which is what you do when you get together to talk and decide about things).

After they had been talking for a while, Romper said, "I'm the oldest elephant in the jungle, and therefore it is up to me to drive these strange men from our jungle and destroy the elephant traps."

"Oh," said the other elephants, "let us go with you to help."

"No," said Romper, "I'm the oldest elephant in the jungle, and I will go."

So Romper started through the jungle to chase away the strange men and destroy the elephant traps. But when he walked, he went ROMP ROMP ROMP ROMP, and the strange men heard him ROMP ROMP ROMPing through the jungle. They quickly finished the elephant trap, set it, and ran into the jungle to hide.

Soon Romper came down the path, and when he saw the elephant trap, he was SO mad that he stepped inside the trap to tear it apart. But, of course, when he stepped inside, the door snapped shut, and Romper was caught in the trap!

The men came rushing from their hiding places in the jungle, pointing their fingers and laughing. "Look, we caught an elephant. See the big elephant we caught." Then they took Romper out of the trap and down the path to their camp and put him in an elephant cage.

When the monkeys and parrots saw what was happening, they raced back through the jungle, crying, "Oh, terrible, *terrible*, terrible, terrible! They've caught Romper! They caught Romper in the elephant trap!"

Tromper, Stomper, and Boo immediately held another conference to decide what to do. Tromper said, "I'm the next oldest elephant in the jungle. It is my duty to rescue Romper, tear down that elephant trap, and chase those men from the jungle."

"We'll come, too," said Stomper and Boo.

"No," Tromper replied, "you wait here."

Tromper started off through the jungle to tear down the elephant trap. But, of course, when she walked through the jungle, she went TROMP TROMP TROMP TROMP, and the men heard her TROMP TROMP TROMPing through the jungle, so they set the trap and ran and hid in the jungle.

Soon Tromper came down the path, and when she saw the trap, it made her so mad that she stepped inside to tear it apart. But when she stepped inside, the door of the trap closed behind her, and Tromper was caught.

The men came racing out of the jungle, pointing their fingers and laughing. "Oh-ho-ho! We caught another elephant!" Then they took Tromper down the path to their camp and put her in a cage beside Romper.

When the monkeys and parrots saw what had happened, they raced back through the treetops, screeching, "Oh, terrible, terrible, *terrible*, terrible! The men have caught Romper *and* Tromper."

When Stomper and Boo heard this, they held a very short conference, because Stomper simply said, "I'm the next oldest elephant in the jungle. It is my duty to rescue Tromper and Romper and destroy the elephant trap and chase those strange men from our jungle." And he set off through the jungle.

But when Stomper walked through the jungle, he went STOMP STOMP STOMP STOMP, and the men heard him STOMP STOMP STOMPing through the jungle, so they quickly set the trap again and ran and hid in the jungle.

Stomper soon came down the path through the jungle, and when he saw the elephant trap, it made him *so* mad that he stepped inside to tear it apart. But when he stepped inside, the door slammed shut behind him, and Stomper was caught in the trap.

The men came racing out of the jungle, pointing their fingers and laughing. "Oh-ho-ho! We caught another elephant!" And they took Stomper down the path to their camp and put him in a cage near Romper and Tromper.

Well, the monkeys and parrots went racing back through the jungle trees, screaming and screeching, "Oh, terrible, terrible, terrible, *terrible!* They have caught Romper,

then Tromper, now Stomper. Boo, what are you going to do?"

"I'm not sure," said Boo, but she set off through the jungle.

Now, remember, when Boo went through the jungle, she didn't make any noise at all. And because she didn't make any noise at all, the strange men didn't hear her coming. And because they didn't hear her coming, they didn't have the elephant trap set. In fact, they were in another part of the jungle, building another elephant trap.

Boo came down the path very quietly, and when she saw that elephant trap, it made her SO angry! But she didn't stop to tear it apart. Instead, she walked around the trap and down the path and was soon at the camp where Romper, Tromper, and Stomper were in cages.

Boo walked up to the cage where Romper was, and she pulled the lock off the door of the cage with her trunk and opened the door of the cage and said, "Boo." "BOO!" said Romper. "Sh-sh!" said Boo and beckoned for Romper to follow her.

Boo and Romper went over to Tromper's cage. Boo pulled the lock off the door, opened it quietly, and said, "Boo." Tromper jumped and said, "BOO!" Boo said, "Sh-sh!" and beckoned with her trunk for Tromper to follow her.

Boo, Romper, and Tromper went over to Stomper's cage, and Boo pulled the lock off the door and opened the door and said, "Boo." Stomper jumped and said, "BOO!" Boo said,

23

"Sh-sh!" and beckoned with her trunk for Stomper to follow her.

All four elephants were going on tiptoe. But four elephants going on tiptoe still make a lot more noise than one elephant on tiptoe, especially if the one elephant is Boo. Still, they were pretty quiet—for elephants—as they followed Boo back down the path toward the elephant trap: ROMP boo TROMP STOMP boo ROMP. When they reached the elephant trap, they were all so mad that they started to tear it apart. Romper grabbed the back of the trap and threw it on the ground and ROMP ROMP ROMP ROMPed on it until there was nothing left but twigs. Tromper grabbed the sides and threw them on the ground and TROMP TROMP TROMP TROMPed on them until there was nothing left of them but toothpicks. Stomper grabbed the roof and threw it on the ground and STOMP STOMP STOMP STOMPed on it until there was nothing left but splinters. And Boo took the front and threw it on the ground and BOO BOO BOO BOOed on it until there was nothing left but dust.

Well, you can imagine what a noise all that ROMPing and TROMPing and STOMPing and even BOOing made! The men heard it way over in the other part of the jungle and came running as fast as they could to find out what was happening. They arrived just in time to find a pile of twigs and toothpicks and splinters and dust and to see four elephants disappearing into the jungle. The men were so discouraged when they realized what had happened that they went away from the jungle and were never seen there again.

Just Old Enough

by RUTH ENGELKEN

When Mark was one, he was just old enough
to walk alone.

> But he was not old enough to play ball
> with big brother Dick,
> or to play hopscotch with sister Lori,
> or to play tag with the kids next door.

When Mark was two, he was just old enough
to wave to the milkman.

> But he was not old enough to bring in
> the milk,
> or to make his own bed,
> or to tie his own shoestrings.

But now Mark is five. And he *is* old enough to go to the big school with Dick and Lori, to count to five—**One**

Two

Three

Four

Five—

to tell red—green—yellow—blue— to fly his own kite, to reach the pedals of a big tricycle, to ride a scooter, to tie his own shoestrings, to make his own bed, to bring in the milk, to play tag with the kids next door, to play hopscotch with Lori, and to play ball with Dick.

It is great to be five.

When Mark was three, he was just old enough to ride a hobbyhorse.

But he was not old enough to ride a scooter, or to reach the pedals of a big tricycle, or to fly his own kite.

When Mark was four, he was just old enough to tell red from green.

But he was not old enough to tell yellow from blue, or to count to five, or to go to kindergarten.

Zoo Riders

by IRMA JOYCE

Look who is riding
   around at the zoo.
Snug in a pouch,
   there's a small kangaroo.

Loons ride on feather beds
   while their folks swim.
Opossums swing upside down—
   what fun for them!

A penguin chick glides
   on Pop's feet over ice.
Koalas ride piggyback—
   isn't that nice?

Upon Mummy's tummy,
   floats junior sea otter.
With help from below,
   hippo calves skim the water.

But here is the best ride
   of all at the zoo—
Away, 'way up high
   on Dad's shoulders ... *guess who!*

The Little Red Hen

as told by JOAN POTTER ELWART

Once upon a time, a Little Red Hen lived in a barnyard with a cat, a dog, and a big fat pig. She was a busy mother hen and spent her days looking for food for her six little chicks.

One day as she was scratching, she found some golden grains of wheat. "Cluck, cluck," she called to her barnyard neighbors. "Who will help me plant this wheat?"

"Not I," said the cat. "I'm too busy doing my thing," and he crouched by a mousehole in the barn.

"Not I," said the dog. "I'd rather play," and he rolled his ball around with his nose.

"Not I," said the pig. "I feel too lazy," he said, as he basked in the warm sunshine.

"Then I will plant the wheat," said the Little Red Hen.

And she did.

When the seeds had grown into tall stalks topped with heavy wheat, the Little Red Hen called to her barnyard neighbors.

"Who will help me cut the wheat?"

"Not I," said the cat, as he watched the

sparrows in the apple tree.

"Not I," said the dog. "I'm having too much fun." He chewed an old shoe, shook it hard, and then tossed it in the air over his head.

"Not I," said the pig. The lazy pig turned over in his mud puddle. "I'm too tired."

"Then I will cut the wheat," said the Little Red Hen.

And she did.

After the Little Red Hen had cut the wheat, she put the grain into a large burlap sack.

"Who will help me take the grain to the mill so the miller can grind it into flour?" she called to her neighbors.

"Not I," said the cat. He was busy doing his cat-thing. He rubbed his soft fur against the ankles of the farmer, hoping the farmer would pour a little of the milk from the pail into his saucer.

"Not I," answered the dog. "This game of

duck-tag is too much fun to leave."

"Not I," said the pig. "I'm resting."

"Then I will take the wheat to the mill," said the Little Red Hen.

And she did.

The Little Red Hen loaded the heavy sack of wheat into a wagon and pulled it down the road to the mill. When she got back to the barnyard, she asked the cat, "Will you help me bake the bread?"

The cat was busy washing the milk off

his whiskers and didn't even answer.

The Little Red Hen called to the dog, as he chased the ducks down the lane. "Will you help me bake the bread?" But the dog was too far away to hear.

Then the Little Red Hen called to the pig: "Will you help me bake the bread?" But the lazy pig had fallen fast asleep.

"Very well," said the Little Red Hen, "then I will bake the bread."

And she did.

The Little Red Hen stirred the yeast and salt and milk into the flour. She kneaded the stretchy dough until the yeast squeaked. Then she patted it into a long white loaf. She set the loaf out in the warm sun to rise. Soon it was as round and plump as the lazy pig's fat belly. Then the Little Red Hen popped the loaf into the oven, and the farmyard was filled with the wonderful smell of fresh bread baking.

"Now, who will help me eat the bread?" clucked the Little Red Hen as she took the golden crusty loaf from the oven.

"I will," said the cat, and he immediately stopped doing his cat-thing and ran to the dinner table.

"I will," said the dog. He quickly forgot the ducks and hurried back to the barn-yard.

"I will," said the pig, and he got to his feet as quickly as a fat pig could.

"Well," said the Little Red Hen. "Who would help me plant the wheat? Who would help me cut the wheat? Who would help me take the wheat to the mill? Who would help me make the bread? No one.

"My chicks and I will eat this bread," said the Little Red Hen.

And they did.

The Girl Who Wanted To Be a Little Red Hen

by MARY HUEY

One sunny summer day there was a little girl who put away her picture book and said to her dolls, "Today I am a little red hen." But her dolls just looked at her and didn't say anything. So she went into the kitchen, where her mother was fixing supper. "Today I am a little red hen," she said.

Her mother just said, "That's nice, dear," and kept on peeling potatoes.

The little girl stomped into the living room and went over to the chair where her daddy was reading the evening paper. "Today I am a little red hen."

"Hmmmm," said her daddy.

She went into her brother's room. "Today I am a little red hen," she shouted.

"Don't step on my cars," said her brother.

The little girl was very unhappy. But the next day she still wanted to play at being a little red hen. When the mailman came to the door, the little girl told him, "Today I am a little red hen."

33

The mailman stepped back and looked at the little girl through the screen door. He took off his hat and scratched the back of his head. "No," he said, "you can't be a little red hen. A little red hen always says 'Cluck, cluck, cluck.'"

The little girl smiled at the mailman. She didn't say anything. But after he had gone, the little girl said "Cluck, cluck, cluck." And all that day whenever she said she was a little red hen she also said "Cluck, cluck, cluck."

The next day when the little girl saw the mailman coming, she rushed to the door. "Today I am a little red hen. Cluck, cluck, cluck," she said proudly.

"Well, now," laughed the mailman, "you certainly do *sound* like a little red hen. But I don't think you are a little red hen. A little red hen flaps its wings and scratches its feet." And the mailman moved his arms up and down and his feet back and forth, looking very much like a big red hen.

All that day the little girl practiced flapping her arms and scratching her feet. It was very hard for her to do, but she tried and tried. And the next day when the mailman came to the door, she was ready.

"Cluck, cluck, cluck," she said. She scratched her feet on the floor and moved her arms up and down. "Today I am a little red hen," she said.

"My, my. You do *look* and *sound* just like a little red hen," chuckled the mailman. "But I thought that little red hens had eggs. You have no eggs. So I guess you aren't a little red hen after all."

That afternoon the little girl went to the kitchen and took an egg from the refrigerator. She carried it to her room and placed it very gently in the lap of her favorite doll.

The next day when the mailman came to the door, the little girl was waiting for him. "I say 'Cluck, cluck, cluck,'" she said. "And I flap my arms and scratch my feet. And," she said as she carefully, oh so carefully, held out the large white egg in her two small hands, "I have an egg. Today I AM A LITTLE RED HEN."

She waited.

"Yes," said the mailman sadly, "I guess you really are a little red hen."

Just as he was saying this, a lady came walking up the sidewalk. "Oh, that's too bad!" she said. "Because I didn't come to see a little red hen. I came to see Lisa."

"Grandma!" shouted the little girl. "I'm not a little red hen anymore. I'm Lisa now."

And so she was.

35

When I Am a Bear

by RUTH ALLISON COATES

When I am a bear,
I will climb a tall tree.

When I am a fish,
I will swim in the sea.

When I am a mole,
I will live in the ground.

When I'm a cricket,
"Chirp-chirp" will I sound.

When I am a bird,
I will fly in the sky.

When I'm a giraffe,
I will stand very high.

When I'm a 'possum,
I will hang upside down.

When I am a cat,
I will roam alleys in town.

When I'm a lion,
I will roar very loud.

When I'm a zebra,
I will draw a big crowd.

When I am a boy (girl)—
But that's what I AM—
Then I'll do all the things
That a boy (girl) can:
    Read . . .
    Laugh . . .
    Think . . .
    Learn . . . .
And whenever I wish,
Pretend I'm a bear . . .
Or a bird . . . or a fish.

The Three Bears

as told by IRMA JOYCE

Once upon a time, in the snuggest house in all the forest, there lived three nice bears— a Papa Bear, a Mamma Bear, and a Baby Bear.

One morning at breakfast, Papa Bear said in his big gruff voice, "My porridge is too hot!"

Then Mamma Bear said in her in-between-sized voice, "*My* porridge is too hot!"

"Ouch!" Baby Bear said in his little squeaky voice. "My porridge is so hot it burns my mouth!"

Papa Bear laid down his spoon. "Why don't we go for a walk?" he said in his big gruff voice. "By the time we get back, our good hot porridge will be cool and ready to eat."

"Let's do that," said Mamma Bear in her in-between-sized voice.

And Baby Bear said in his squeaky little voice, "Yes, let's."

So off they went for a stroll in the forest.

Now, the three bears didn't know it, but there was somebody else nearby. A somebody else with curls the color of new gold. And she was called Goldilocks.

When Goldilocks reached the bears' house, she felt lonesome because she had not met any girls or boys to play with. "Maybe some children live here," she said, and she knocked on the door.

Of course, no one answered. And so Goldilocks opened the door and walked into the little house.

The first thing she saw was Papa Bear's big bowl of porridge. It looked so tasty that she tried a big spoonful.

"Oh, this porridge is too hot!" she said.

So then she tried the porridge in the in-between-sized bowl.

"Oh, this porridge is too cold!" she said.

At last she tried the porridge in the little bowl. "This porridge is just right," she said, and she ate it all up. Every bit.

Since Goldilocks had walked a long way in the forest, she felt like sitting down.

Near the fireplace stood three chairs—a big sturdy chair, a middle-sized ruffly sort of chair, and a little polka-dotted chair.

Goldilocks sat in the big sturdy chair.

But it was much too hard.

So then she sat in the in-between-sized ruffly sort of chair.

But it was much too soft.

Last of all she sat in the little polka-dotted chair.

It seemed to be just right. But it wasn't just right. For suddenly the little chair broke into pieces. And Goldilocks sat down hard upon the floor.

"I'll have to try to put it back together," she said sadly. "But first I must have a nap."

And so she climbed the stairs that led to the bedroom. There she saw three beds—a great big one, a middle-sized one, and a very small one.

First she tried Papa Bear's bed. But, "This big bed is much too hard," she said.

So then she tried Mamma Bear's bed. But, "This in-between-sized bed is much too soft," she said.

Last of all she tried Baby Bear's bed. "This little bed is just right," she murmured. In no time at all, she was fast asleep.

It wasn't long before the three bears came home from their walk in the forest and hurried into the house for breakfast.

Papa Bear said loudly, "Somebody's been eating my porridge!"

Mamma Bear said in-betweenly, "Somebody's been eating *my* porridge!"

Baby Bear said squeakily, "Somebody's been eating mine, too, and has eaten it all up!"

"Hmmm," said Papa Bear. "Let's sit down and think about this."

"Let's do that," said Mamma Bear.

"Yes, let's," said Baby Bear.

And so they went to their chairs near the fireplace.

Now, Papa Bear knew someone had been sitting in his chair because it was too far *off* the rug.

Mamma Bear knew someone had been sitting in her chair because it was too far *on* the rug.

Poor Baby Bear! He knew someone had been sitting in his chair because it was *all over the rug!*

"Well, now," said Papa Bear. "Perhaps we just better look upstairs."

"Let's do that," said Mamma Bear.

"Yes, let's," said Baby Bear. "But I'll go last."

With the biggest, bravest bear leading the way, they tiptoed upstairs.

"Look!" whispered Papa Bear. "Somebody's been sleeping in my bed!"

"Look! Look!" whispered Mamma Bear. "Somebody's been sleeping in *my* bed!"

"Look! Look! Look!" said Baby Bear, forgetting to whisper. "Somebody's been sleeping in my bed—and here she is!"

With that, Goldilocks woke up and saw the three bears standing around her.

"Bears!" she cried. "Fierce, hungry bears!"

Then she jumped up, dashed down the stairs, and ran out of the house.

The three bears looked at each other and smiled.

Silly girl! They weren't fierce bears, not the least bit.

But Goldilocks was right about one thing. They were *hungry* bears.

So with Baby Bear leading the way, they all went down to the kitchen and enjoyed a fresh helping of good just-right porridge.

The 621 Friends of Aaron Zee

by ANN TOMPERT

In a little gray house by the side of the road, there once lived a little old man whose name was Aaron Zee. Although he liked his house, Aaron Zee was unhappy because he lived all alone.

"I know what I'll do," said Aaron Zee one day. "I'll find someone to live with me."

So he put up a sign.

I NEED A FRIEND

By and by, a white horse came along. He had no master, as he was too old to work. He read the sign and decided to be friends with Aaron Zee.

How happy Aaron Zee was as he sat on his front porch, watching the horse chomp grass.

After a while, a brown cow came by.

"I'm running away because they want to sell me to the butcher," said the cow.

"Come live with us," said the horse.

And Aaron Zee danced a jig when the cow agreed to stay.

The next day, a black and white sheep joined the horse and cow.

"What extraordinary luck to have three friends!" exclaimed Aaron Zee.

A few days later, a little dog joined them. Aaron Zee was so happy he turned a somersault.

"Four friends!" he cried. "I'll never be lonely again."

The following week, three pigs made their home under the front porch.

"Seven are quite enough friends for me," said Aaron Zee.

And he took down his sign.

But word had spread far and wide that all were welcome to live with Aaron Zee. Every day more and more animals came.

A donkey and seven cats moved into the living room.

A fox, a raccoon, and five little skunks took over the kitchen cupboards.

A duck swam in the sink.

Nine monkeys swung from the rafters in the attic.

And a squirrel made her nest in the chimney.

When the hunting season opened, ten brown rabbits, nineteen white rabbits, and twenty-one black rabbits scampered to the little gray house.

A dozen rabbits settled under the kitchen table. Two dozen went under the dining-room table. And the rest went under the tables in the living room.

Aaron Zee counted and found he had eighty-three friends.

"No room for more," he said.

He put up another sign. But no one bothered to read this sign.

A flock of thirty-eight chickens invaded the little gray house. They roosted on the windowsills and lamps and on the bookcases.

"One hundred and twenty-one," cried Aaron Zee. "That's enough!"

But more and more came.

One hundred and fifty mice moved into the kitchen stove.

Thirty-seven birds nested in the pots and pans.

Three hundred turtles came. They crawled into the fireplace and under Aaron Zee's bed. They even crawled into his slippers.

Eleven opossums filled the chest of drawers.

When an otter came to play in Aaron Zee's bathtub, there were 620 creatures in the little gray house.

And when a bear who snored took over his bed, Aaron Zee had 621 friends! BUT HE WAS NO LONGER HAPPY.

"Too many friends living too close is worse than no friends at all," said Aaron Zee.

One by one he bade them good-bye. Then he set out to find a new house.

He had not gone very far when he found a little red house where no one lived. As soon as he moved in, he turned a dozen cartwheels, because he was so happy to be living by himself again.

Of course, there were times when Aaron Zee felt lonesome. And when he did, he had 621 friends to visit in the little gray house by the side of the road.

Hello, Sun

by FLORENCE M. WHITE

Hello, Sun.
Hello, Day.
Did you wake me up to play?

Hello, Dog.
Hello, Cat.
Come here and play upon my mat.

Hello, Butterfly.
Hello, Bee.
Will you come and play with me?

Hello, Earthworm.
Hello, Snail.
Come and see what's in my pail.

Hello, Squirrel.
Hello, Deer.
Come and play with me right here.

Hello, Robin.
Hello, Jay.
Do you also want to play?

Hello, Rooster.
Hello, Hen.
Will you play with me again?

Hello,
Little, little Mouse.
Will you come out of your house?

Hello, David.
Hello, May.
Come let's have a happy day.

Hello, hello,
Everyone.
Come and we'll have lots of fun.

Erik and Red
and the Store

A Toddler's Tale by BETTY KENT

Erik is a boy. Red is a squirrel.

Erik lives downstairs in a big yellow house.
Red lives in a walnut tree in Erik's backyard.

One cold day the pink telephone rang.
Mamma put the phone to her ear.

Erik got his blue telephone. He put his
phone to his ear. He sat near the window
and pretended to listen.

After a while, Mamma put the pink phone
down. "Come, Erik," she said, "we must go
to the store. Grandma is coming for lunch."

"Car?" said Erik, running for his coat.

"Daddy has the car today," Mamma said. "We will take the bike."

Erik liked the bike. There was a seat for him behind Mamma. She fastened the strap around him so he couldn't fall out.

Mamma's feet went around and around on the pedals. The wheels went around and around, too.

The wind blew Erik's yellow hair. The wind blew Mamma's brown hair. And they rode to the store.

There were many cars and bikes around the store. Mamma put the bike in the rack.

She took the strap off Erik and lifted him down. Erik held Mamma's hand.

The store was full of people. It was full of things to buy, too. Mamma bought bread, and then they went outside again.

Mamma put Erik back into his bike seat. She put the strap around him so he couldn't fall out. "Can you carry the bread?" she asked.

"I can," said Erik, holding it very carefully.

Mamma made the pedals go around and around. The wheels went around and around, too. The wind blew Erik's yellow hair. The wind blew Mamma's brown hair. And they rode back home.

When they got home, Mamma took the strap off Erik. She lifted him down.

Erik gave Mamma the bread. And then he saw Red. Red was digging in Mamma's flower bed.

Erik could dig only in his sandbox.

"Naughty Red, naughty Red," Erik said, pointing to Red.

"No," Mamma said. "Red isn't naughty. Red is hungry. He is digging for a nut he put there last summer. The flower bed is Red's store."

Erik had a store. He was glad Red had a store, too.

And then Erik went into the house to help Mamma. Grandma was coming for lunch, you know.

Little Red Riding Hood

as told by IRMA JOYCE

Once upon a time, long, long ago when scary animals ran around loose, there lived a little girl called Little Red Riding Hood.

One day Little Red Riding Hood's mother said, "Dear, please take this basket of goodies to Grandmother. Don't linger along the way, and watch out for the wolf in the woods."

Red Riding Hood promised to be careful. She put on her little red cape. Then she picked up the basket of goodies and started down the path through the woods.

She hadn't gone far when someone jumped out from behind a tree—someone with big wicked eyes, long pointed ears, and *very* sharp teeth!

"Hel-lo," said the wolf, pretending to be nice. "Stop and show me what's in your pretty basket, my dear."

But Little Red Riding Hood remembered what her mother had said. "Oh, no. This basket of goodies is for Grandma," she said. "And I may not linger along the way." I must hurry to Grandma's house."

"Very wise," said the wolf. "Now, my dear, why don't we just race and see who gets to Grandma's first. You go your way and I'll go mine."

49

And so Little Red Riding Hood, staying on the path, hurried to Grandma's house.

But the wolf knew a secret path. He hurried through the woods, and he got to Grandma's house first.

He knocked on the door and called in a high, singsongy voice, "Let me in, Grandmamma. It's Little Red Riding Hood and I've brought you a basket of goodies."

"Lift the latch and walk in, dear," called Grandma. "For I'm in bed, quite unwell."

And so the wolf lifted the latch and walked in.

He locked Grandma in the closet.

He found her frilliest nightcap and put it on.

Then he hopped into her puffy feather bed just as Little Red Riding Hood knocked on the door.

"Grandma, are you home?" called Little Red Riding Hood.

"Yes," called the wolf in a shaky, quaky voice. "But I'm quite unwell today. Lift the latch and walk in, dear."

And so Little Red Riding Hood lifted the latch and walked in.

"What a pretty basket of goodies," said the wolf in his sweetest voice. "Bring it here, dear child."

As Little Red Riding Hood went near the bed, she said, "My, what big eyes you have, Grandma."

The wolf said, "The better to see you with, my dear."

Then Red Riding Hood said, "My, what long pointed ears you have, Grandma."

The wolf answered, "The better to hear you with, my dear."

"My," said Red Riding Hood, "what sharp teeth you have, Grandma."

"The better to eat you with!" laughed the wolf, and he leaped out of bed.

But before he could catch her, Little Red Riding Hood scrambled under the table.

"Help!" she called. "Oh, help. The wolf is here!"

At that very moment some big strong woodchoppers happened to be passing by. They heard Little Red Riding Hood and ran to the cottage.

When the wolf heard them coming, he jumped out the window and ran into the forest.

Swinging their axes, the woodchoppers ran after him.

The wolf was never seen in that part of the woods again, and it became a good place to play.

Little Red Riding Hood always played there on nice days.

And she always laughed when she remembered someone with big eyes . . . long ears . . . and a silly, frilly nightcap.

51

I Went to the Zoo in the Rain

by BETTY LACEY

I put on my raincoat. I put on my rain boots.
I put on my rain hat. I took my umbrella
and I went to the zoo in the rain, rain,
RAIN! IN THE SHOWERING,
TINGLING, DRIZZLING RAIN! IN
THE TRICKLING, SPLASHING,
DRIPPING RAIN! IN THE BUBBLING,
SOAKING, SLOSHING RAIN! IN
THE POURING, SPRINKLING,
DRENCHING RAIN!

Showering Rain!

The elephant was taking a bath in the
SHOWERING rain. He used his trunk to
scrub his back and wash behind his ears.

Tingling Rain!

The TINGLING rain was splashing on the hippopotamus' tongue. I wondered if it tickled his teeth.

Drizzling Rain!

The bear slept curled up in the DRIZZLING rain. He looked like a big, soft fur pillow. He was snoring out loud.

Trickling Rain!

The TRICKLING rain ran down the camel's ears. He looked so sad that I gave him my rain hat. Then he smiled.

Splashing Rain!

The gorilla was doing a dance in the SPLASHING rain. He loved to jump up and down in the puddles.

Dripping Rain!

The giraffe hid his head in a tree while his back got wet in the DRIPPING rain. I gave him my raincoat. I think it was too small.

Bubbling Rain!

The ducks swam around in the BUBBLING rain in the pond. They were quacking happily. The ducks like the rain.

Soaking Rain!

The ostrich's feet got very wet in the SOAKING rain. I gave him my rain boots. They did not fit very well.

Sloshing Rain!

The zebra walked slowly through the SLOSHING rain. He was looking for green grass to nibble.

Pouring Rain!

The monkeys hid in the monkey cave. They did not want to get wet in the POURING rain. I could see their little eyes peeking out.

Sprinkling Rain!

The alligator slept in the pond. He did not even feel the SPRINKLING rain.

Drenching Rain!

The lion did not like the DRENCHING rain. I gave him my umbrella. It kept him dry, except for his tail.

Then, without my hat, without my boots, without my coat, without my umbrella, I walked home from the zoo in the SHOWERING, TINGLING, DRIZZLING, TRICKLING, SPLASHING, DRIPPING, BUBBLING, SOAKING, SLOSHING, POURING, SPRINKLING, DRENCHING

RAIN!!

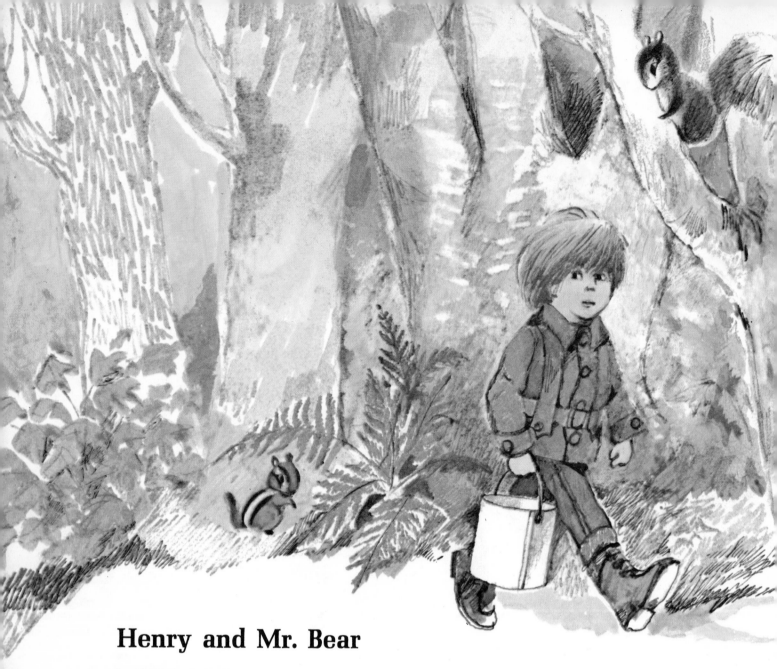

Henry and Mr. Bear

by HELEN KRONBERG OLSON

Once upon a time, there was a little boy and his name was Henry. Henry lived at the edge of a deep, deep forest. In the forest grew wild berries.

One day Henry became hungry for juicy, ripe wild berries. "There is only one thing for me to do," said Henry.

So he put on his green jacket, buttoned up his green buttons, and away he hurried into the forest.

All the while he walked, he kept a sharp lookout for Mr. Bear. Everyone knew Mr. Bear lived in the forest. And everyone knew he liked nothing better than to gobble things up. But Henry got all the way to the first berry patch without seeing Mr. Bear.

Many berry bushes grew in the first berry patch. But even though Henry looked and looked in the bushes, not one single berry did he find.

Henry saw a lone raccoon sitting nearby. The raccoon was fanning himself with a leaf.

"Good-day, Raccoon," said Henry.

"Good-day," said the raccoon, as he politely put down his leaf.

"Where have all the berries gone?" asked Henry.

"Mr. Bear was here yesterday," said the raccoon. "And he gobbled them all up."

"There is only one thing for me to do," said Henry. "I will go farther into the forest to the second berry patch."

"Watch out for Mr. Bear," said the raccoon. "If he catches you, he will gobble you up, too."

"I will take care," said Henry.

And he did get all the way to the second berry patch without seeing Mr. Bear.

Many berry bushes grew in the second berry patch. But even though Henry looked and looked, he could not find one berry there either.

Henry saw a lone fox sitting nearby. The fox was picking his teeth with a twig.

"Good-day, Fox," said Henry.

"Good-day," said the fox, as he politely laid his twig aside.

"Where have all the berries gone?" asked Henry.

"Mr. Bear was here this morning," said the fox. "And he gobbled them all up."

"There is only one thing for me to do," said Henry. "I will go farther into the forest to the third berry patch."

"Watch out for Mr. Bear," the fox said. "If he catches you, he will gobble you up, too."

"I will take care," said Henry.

By now he was so hungry for berries that he ran all the way to the next patch.

And there, at the last patch in the forest, Henry could see many juicy, ripe berries. The bushes were loaded with them.

But there—there was Mr. Bear at the other end of the patch. And he was gobbling down berries as fast as he could.

Henry watched him from behind a tree.

"Mr. Bear will have to stop eating soon," he thought, "or he will surely burst."

But Mr. Bear did not slow down in his eating. Nor did he look up.

Finally Henry became so hungry he could not stand it one minute more. "I will tiptoe over to the nearest bush and eat just one berry," he said to himself.

In a twinkling he was standing in front of the bush. Quickly he picked one juicy berry and popped it into his mouth.

It was so good that he picked another and another. Before he knew it, he had forgotten all about Mr. Bear. And he was eating berries as fast as he could.

Then he saw the largest ripest berry of all. It hung high on the bush. His hand reached for the berry.

At the same time, a huge furry paw reached for the very same berry.

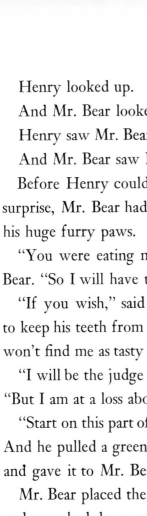

Henry looked up.

And Mr. Bear looked down.

Henry saw Mr. Bear.

And Mr. Bear saw Henry.

Before Henry could let out one squeak of surprise, Mr. Bear had grabbed him in both his huge furry paws.

"You were eating my berries," said Mr. Bear. "So I will have to gobble you up."

"If you wish," said Henry, as he tried to keep his teeth from chattering. "But you won't find me as tasty as ripe, juicy berries."

"I will be the judge of that," said Mr. Bear. "But I am at a loss about where to start."

"Start on this part of me first," said Henry. And he pulled a green button off his jacket and gave it to Mr. Bear.

Mr. Bear placed the button in his mouth and crunched down on it.

He made a funny face and spit out the button.

"If that one doesn't please you," said Henry, "you must try another." He pulled the next button from his jacket and gave it to Mr. Bear.

Mr. Bear stuck this button in his mouth, too, and crunched down. He spit this one out even faster than the first.

After he had tried three more buttons, he looked at Henry sadly and shook his head. "I hate to tell you this," said Mr. Bear, "but the truth of the matter is you are still too green to eat."

Then he let go of Henry.

"There is only one thing for me to do," said Henry.

And away he ran—

Out of the forest—

To his own little home—

To sew more green buttons on his jacket.

"Just in case I meet Mr. Bear again," said Henry.

But he never did.